MAD

KT-427-333

C334357823

For Olivia Perkes, who would be a perfect Star Friend,
and for the lovely Sandra Jimminson for all her help –
and that pitchfork suggestion! – LC

STRIPES PUBLISHING LIMITED
An imprint of the Little Tiger Group
1 Coda Studios, 189 Munster Road,
London SW6 6AW

A paperback original
First published in Great Britain in 2019

Text copyright © Linda Chapman, 2019
Illustrations © Lucy Fleming and Mike Love, 2019

ISBN: 978-1-78895-037-4

Printed and bound in the UK.

2 4 6 8 10 9 7 5 3 1

Star Friends
MOONLIGHT MISCHIEF

LINDA CHAPMAN
ILLUSTRATED BY LUCY FLEMING

In the Star World

The hills and valleys were coated with stardust
and the trees in the forest glittered and shone.
A silver wolf stood beside a peaceful forest
pool with a large owl perched on her back.
They were watching a picture on the surface
of the water. The image was dark around the
edges but in the centre they could see a girl
with blond hair snuggled up in bed, holding
a fox cub in her arms. The fox opened his
indigo eyes and began licking the girl's nose.
She woke up and giggled.

"Maia and Bracken," said the owl softly.

"They love each other very much indeed," said the wolf. A wistful look crossed her face. "I wish Maia's granny could have seen them together. She would have been so happy to know that her granddaughter had become a Star Friend – just like she did when she was younger."

"I hope Maia, Bracken and their friends do as much good as her granny and you did, Silver," said the owl.

The wolf nodded. "I am sure they will. Since the girls became Star Friends, they have done an excellent job of keeping Westcombe village safe."

Every so often, animals from the magical Star World would travel down to the human world to find a girl or boy to be their Star Friend. They taught them how to connect with the magical current that ran between the two worlds. When a child became a Star Friend, they and their animal bonded for life, using magic to do good – helping people around them to be happy and stopping anyone using dark magic.

"Do you see the black cloud at the edge of the image?" said the owl. "It looks like dark magic is coming to Westcombe again."

"Maia and her friends will be ready for it," declared the wolf as they watched Maia throw back her duvet and jump out of bed with Bracken bounding happily round her legs.

The owl hooted. "I hope so. Let us watch and see."

Chapter One

Maia giggled. "Try again, Bracken! Try harder!"

She was sitting on the floor with a magical silvery bubble surrounding her like a dome. Bracken leaped at it but he simply bounced off it, landing on Maia's bedroom rug. He jumped back up and scrabbled at the sides with his paws. The dome wobbled slightly but didn't break.

Giving up, he sank back down on his haunches. "You're getting really good at making magic shields, Maia," he said, panting. "I can't get through at all."

Maia grinned and disconnected from the
magic current – it was like flicking a switch off
in her mind. The tingling buzz of magic slowly
faded from her blood and the bubble vanished.
Bracken bounded forwards and sprang on to
her lap. She wrapped her arms round him,
burying her face in his soft russet-red fur. She
loved him so much. She'd only been a Star
Friend for six months but already she could
hardly remember life before Bracken and
magic.

"It's really fun being able to make shields,"
she said. "And it might be useful if we have to

fight another Shade."

Shades were evil spirits conjured by people using dark magic. They brought misery and chaos. Star Friends, like Maia, had to use magic to stop them and send them back to the Shadows where they belonged.

"Why don't you use your seeing magic to find out if there is anything we should be investigating at the moment?" said Bracken.

"OK." Maia jumped to her feet and picked up a small mirror from her desk. Cupping it in her hands, she sat back down and gazed into the shining surface, opening herself to the current again. It tingled and sparked through her, like faint pins and needles in every cell of her body. Star Friends all had different magical abilities and Maia was able to use the magic to look into the past and future, to see things that were happening elsewhere and to get warnings from the magic if danger was coming. "Show me if there's anything we should be worried about," she whispered.

Her reflection faded in the glass and a new image appeared. It showed the main road that led into the village of Westcombe – the village where Maia and her friends lived. The image dissolved and was replaced by a different picture – a cluster of cottages, one covered in ivy that looked vaguely familiar. It quickly changed again, this time showing the back of a woman with short brown hair who was examining her reflection in a mirror with lights round it. There was something odd about the reflection – something that didn't seem quite right – but before Maia could work out what it was the image changed once more and she caught a glimpse of a small black shape – a phone or maybe a TV remote? Maia blinked in surprise. Why was the magic showing her a TV remote? But, before she could look more closely, the surface of the mirror cleared and all she saw was her own reflection again.

Maia told Bracken what she had seen. "I don't know what the pictures mean. I didn't see anything really scary like a Shade or someone doing dark magic. Just a road, a woman, something that looked like a remote control and some cottages."

Bracken scratched his nose with a front paw. "The magic will have shown you those things for a reason. I wonder why."

Unease prickled through Maia. "I'd better tell the others so we can keep an eye out in case anything strange starts to happen."

Her best friends, Lottie, Sita and Ionie, were all Star Friends, too. They each had their own

Star Animal – Ionie's was a wildcat called Sorrel, Lottie's was a red squirrel called Juniper and Sita's was a gentle fallow deer called Willow.

"Are we meeting up after school today?" Bracken asked.

"Yes. Ionie's asked us all round to her house for tea but we'll come to the clearing first," said Maia.

The clearing was in the woods near Ionie's house. The girls often went there because it was a beautiful place of very powerful magic. Hardly anyone else ever visited the clearing, which meant it was a safe place where they could practise magic with their animals. The Star Animals tried not to be seen by other humans – the Star World had to be kept secret from anyone who wasn't a Star Friend.

"Maia! Breakfast!" her mum called from the kitchen.

"Coming, Mum! I'll just get dressed! I'd

better go," she told Bracken, pulling on her school clothes. She gave him a quick hug. "I'll see you later."

"I'll miss you," Bracken said, licking her cheek. "Meet me as soon as you can."

"I will." Maia kissed his fluffy head and went downstairs.

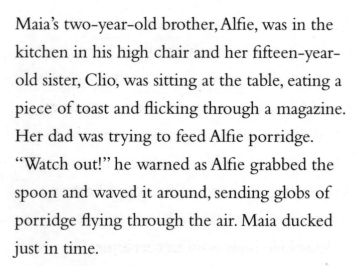

Maia's two-year-old brother, Alfie, was in the kitchen in his high chair and her fifteen-year-old sister, Clio, was sitting at the table, eating a piece of toast and flicking through a magazine. Her dad was trying to feed Alfie porridge. "Watch out!" he warned as Alfie grabbed the spoon and waved it around, sending globs of porridge flying through the air. Maia ducked just in time.

"No, Alfie, you mustn't do that," said Mr Greene. Alfie chuckled and hit him on the head with his plastic spoon.

Maia bit back a grin. She knew she shouldn't giggle when Alfie was being naughty but sometimes it was very hard not to.

"So what's happening at school today?" her dad asked as Maia poured herself some cereal.

"Not much, just spelling and times-tables tests."

"Lucky you," said Clio, looking up enviously. "I've got double maths, physics and French. I wish I was still in Year Six."

"Miss Harris also said Lottie, Ionie, Sita and I could help with some gardening at lunchtime," said Maia. "The flower bed by the Reception classroom is full of weeds and we're going to clear it so Reception can plant some summer flowers there."

"Then remember to put sunscreen on before you go to school, and take a hat," said her dad. "It's supposed to be very warm today."

Maia glanced out of the window at the blue sky. The last week had been very sunny. It was great now the weather was getting warmer and the nights lighter – it made it much easier for her and the others to meet up after school.

"I can't wait for the Easter holidays," said Maia.

"What are you two going to do with all that free time?" her dad said.

"Revise, see friends and sleep!" Clio yawned.

Maia listed her plans. "Sleepovers, swimming, maybe go to the cinema, play on the beach, paddle in the sea, get ice creams from the Copper Kettle…"

She smiled to herself as she added in her head, *And do lots of magic, too, of course!*

CHAPTER TWO

"I do like gardening," said Sita happily. "This bed is going to look so much better with flowers in it." It was lunchtime and she, Maia, Ionie and Lottie were kneeling on mats by the flower bed in a quiet spot outside the Reception children's classroom, pulling up weeds and turning the soil over.

"It's so hot," said Lottie, pushing back her dark curls and fanning her face.

"It's the hottest day of the year so far," Ionie informed them. "In fact, this is the hottest

March on record." She sat back on her heels. "It's been hotter here than in Spain this month. The average temperature in Westcombe has been— Ow!" She broke off as a thorn in the soil caught her wrist above the top of her gloves and scratched her skin. "That hurt!" she said, shaking her wrist and looking at the droplets of blood blooming in a line on her skin.

"Here," said Sita quickly. Reaching over, she took Ionie's wrist in her hands and shut her eyes. She breathed in and out slowly. The blood on Ionie's pale skin vanished and the scratch healed to a pink line that gradually faded away completely. Sita opened her eyes. "Better?"

"Much," said Ionie. "Thank you."

"Your magic is awesome," Lottie told Sita.

Like Maia, the other girls could use the magic current to do different things. As well as healing, Sita had the ability to command people to do as she said, although she didn't like that power and only used it when she really had to. Lottie could run fast and be very agile. Ionie could shadow-travel and disguise things, and she was also a Spirit Speaker, which meant she could send Shades back to the Shadows where they belonged.

"I can't wait to meet up with the animals and do some magic together later," said Lottie. "I'm so glad I've got an afternoon with no activities for once."

Lottie did lots of things after school and at the weekend – gymnastics, piano, flute, tennis, maths and French – which made it difficult for her to meet up with the others.

"How come you've got tonight off?" Maia

asked her.

"Mum is letting me stop my extra maths lessons now I've passed the entrance exam for the High School," Lottie said.

"It's going to be strange being at different schools in September," said Sita. "We'll be at King John Academy and you'll be at the High School."

"You will all stay friends with me, won't you?" Lottie asked anxiously.

"Of course not," Maia teased. "We can't possibly be friends with you if you're at a different school."

But Lottie didn't smile as Maia had expected. She bit her lip and looked down at her hands.

"I didn't mean it," Maia said quickly. She hadn't for one second thought Lottie might take her seriously. "Of course we'll stay friends."

"So, if you're not doing maths now, does that mean you'll have every Monday night free?" Ionie said, not seeming to notice that

Lottie was looking upset.

Lottie shrugged. "No such luck. It's just this week. I'm starting Spanish lessons next week."

"But you already speak German, what with your dad being German, *and* you're learning French," said Ionie.

"I know but apparently –" Lottie mimicked her mum's voice – "*learning a new language is so much easier when you're younger.* I can hardly say I want Mondays off so I can go and do magic." She sighed. "I wish I didn't have to do so many activities and I could meet up with you more."

"At least we've got the Easter holidays coming up," said Sita. "That'll give us lots of extra time together."

"Lots of time to use magic to do good and help people!" Maia said.

"And maybe fight Shades," said Ionie, her green eyes sparkling.

Sita shuddered. "I don't know why you sound so excited about that! I'd be happy if I never saw a Shade ever again."

There were different types of Shades but they all liked to make people unhappy and miserable – either by talking to them and twisting their thoughts or by making bad things happen. Maia and the others had had to fight quite a few Shades since they had become Star Friends. Bad people had used dark magic to trap Shades in everyday objects like mirrors or toys so that they could get them into other people's houses.

"Do you remember those last Shades? The ones in the dreamcatchers that made all the grown-ups they affected become really competitive?" said Maia. She pictured the Shades they had released from the dreamcatchers – tall, thin and shadowy with spiny fingers and glowing red eyes.

"And there was that one trapped in the garden gnome," said Sita. "The Wish Shade. Do you remember how he locked me and Lottie in a shed and set fire to it? We could have burned to death! They're so dangerous!"

"*Shh,*" Ionie said quickly as Lucia, one of the Reception children, skipped over to them.

"Maia!" the little girl squealed, throwing her arms round Maia's waist. "I've been looking for you!" At Westcombe Primary School, the little Reception children were all assigned a buddy from Year Six. Maia was Lucia's buddy.

"Hi, Lucia," said Maia, hugging her back.

"What are you doing?" asked Lucia as she wriggled free from the hug.

"Sorting this flower bed out so your class can plant some flowers in it and it'll look pretty again," said Maia.

Lucia beamed. "Nana and Grandpa will be pleased. They said we have to make the school look as nice as possible so Westcombe wins the prize in the village competition. Nana's coming into assembly to talk to everyone about it this afternoon."

"Lucia's nana is Ana-Lucia Jefferson – one of the school governors," Maia explained to the others.

Understanding dawned on their faces. They often saw Ana-Lucia, or Ana as she was usually called, about the school. She worked as a lawyer four days a week but on her day off she came in and listened to reading in the younger classes. She was always very smiley and friendly. She was married to Mike, who had lived in the village all his life and was on the Parent Teacher Association, and involved with lots of village fund-raising events.

"What's the competition for?" Ionie said. She liked any sort of competition.

"It's for Best Kept Village," said Sita. "My dad was telling me about it. All the villages around here can enter. Westcombe won it a few years ago."

"Nana and Grandpa really want Westcombe to win again this year," said Lucia. "They're moving to Portugal after the summer when Nana retires. Grandpa said he would really love to see Westcombe win once more before they go."

"Maybe we can help tidy the village up," said Lottie.

"That's what Nana's going to talk about in assembly," said Lucia. She threw her arms wide. "She wants *everyone* to help."

The bell rang in the playground.

"Time to pack up," said Sita.

Lucia ran off to line up with her class while Maia and the others put the gardening

equipment away in the shed and hurried inside
to wash their hands.

✦ ✦ ✦

"So, if all of you could help Westcombe try
and win the Best Kept Village competition, it
would be absolutely fantastic!" Ana Jefferson
said as she finished her talk in assembly.

Lucia's nana had dark brown, sleek, chin-
length hair with some strands of silvery grey.
Her voice had a faint accent – she had lived in
Westcombe for many years but had grown up
in Portugal.

"The competition is being judged in a
week's time. We need gardens to be tidy, litter
to be picked up, the school to look spick and
span. If everyone joins in and works together,
I'm sure we can manage it. Can I count on you
all to help?"

Everyone nodded.

"It's a great idea," said Mrs King, the

headteacher, standing up. "Why don't all classes use the time between now and the end of school to have a think about what they can do?"

Assembly ended and for the rest of the afternoon the two Year Six classes made posters to put up around the village telling people about the competition and asking them to keep everywhere tidy.

Maia really enjoyed designing her poster although on the next-door table some of the more annoying boys in her class – Dan, Nikhil and Josh – were moaning.

"This is so boring," Dan said.

"Yeah, who wants to make dumb posters for some stupid contest," agreed Josh, putting his pen down.

"I'm not tidying up the village," said Nikhil, abandoning his poster and sticking his arms behind his head.

"Come on, boys," said Miss Harris, walking over. "Get on with your posters."

They reluctantly picked up their pens again but, as she walked off, Maia heard them muttering together again.

"Stupid contest."

Everyone else, however, seemed keen to finish their posters and make plans to help. The afternoon passed quickly and Maia was almost sad when school finished – but then she remembered that she and the others were going to the clearing to meet up with the animals and do magic!

It was lovely to leave the stuffy classroom and get out into the fresh air. Ionie turned her face to the sun. "Let's ask my dad if we can get ice creams from the Copper Kettle on the way home. It's definitely an ice-cream day."

"Every day should be an ice-cream day," Maia declared. Mary, who ran the Copper Kettle café, made the best home-made ice cream ever!

They ran over to where Ionie's dad was talking to Ana and Mike, a tall, slim balding man, who had an air of energy and enthusiasm about him. Lucia was with them. She had an old red shoebox in her arms.

"It's the PTA fortune-telling evening tonight," Mike was saying to Ionie's dad. "Are you coming along?"

Ionie's dad chuckled. "It's not my cup of tea. You don't really believe in things like that, do you, Mike?"

"Oh, he does," said Ana, shaking her head affectionately at her husband. "The horoscopes are the first thing he looks at it in the paper every morning."

"You may laugh but I believe that it's good to keep an open mind." Mike smiled. "Maybe this fortune-teller really can see into the future." He turned to Maia. "Your mum's coming along, isn't she, Maia?"

Maia nodded.

"Lucia's staying over with us tonight," said Ana. "So, if you'd like to come round, Maia, then please do. Lucia would love to have someone to play with while the fortune-telling is going on."

"Come round, Maia. *Pleeease!*" begged Lucia.

"OK," Maia said. "I'm going to Ionie's house now but I'll come over with Mum later."

As Ionie started to ask her dad if they could stop at the Copper Kettle, Lucia showed the box she was holding to Maia. "Look what I brought in for show-and-tell today!"

She opened the lid to reveal two large dolls with dark hair – a man and a woman. The

female doll was wearing a heavy black skirt
with an embroidered
apron and black plastic
oval-shaped shoes, and
had a basket of plastic
fruit on her head.
The male doll was
a shepherd with
a red waistcoat,
black knee-length
trousers, a green
hat a bit like
an elf's and a
wooden shepherd's crook
in his hands.

"They're Nana's. Do you like them?" asked
Lucia.

Maia didn't really like dolls much and these
two had creepy glass eyes that blinked as Lucia
moved the box. However, she didn't want to be
rude. "They're … um … lovely."

"When I was little, I used to collect dolls in traditional dress from different countries," said Ana. "My father used to travel quite a lot and he would buy them for me. These were my first two dolls – they're Portuguese."

"Like you, Nana," said Lucia.

Ana smiled. "Yes, just like me."

"It's not long until you move to Portugal, is it?" Ionie's dad said.

"No, end of the summer," said Mike. "I've been practising my Portuguese. Luckily it's pretty similar to Spanish and I'm fluent in that."

Just then, Lottie and Sita came hurrying out of their cloakroom – they were in a different Year Six class to Maia and Ionie. "Sorry we're late. We were just finishing our posters," said Sita.

"Can we walk home via the Copper Kettle, Dad?" Ionie asked. "It's such a nice day – perfect for ice cream!"

"Well, I have got the car but you can walk if

you want to and I'll meet you at home. Here's some money for ice creams"

"Thank you!" the girls chorused,

"See you later, Lucia," Maia called as she set off with the others. It was time for some magic — and fun!

CHAPTER THREE

As the girls walked through Westcombe's pretty winding streets, past the village green and duck pond, they saw a few of the older members of the village out and about, weeding the churchyard and planting flowers round the edge of the village green. The sun seemed to be making everyone cheerful, and people smiled at them and said hello as they passed.

"Everyone's really getting involved with tidying up, aren't they?" said Lottie. "We should offer to help at the weekend."

"We could use magic!" Ionie suggested.

"But I don't see how any of our magic powers can help," said Maia.

Ionie's green eyes sparkled. She cast a quick look around and then stared at an old bench near them. It changed from tatty-looking to brand-new.

"Ionie, stop it!" Lottie hissed in alarm. "Someone might see!"

Ionie grinned and the illusion faded. "Don't worry, Miss Sensible. No one was watching."

Maia saw Lottie's mouth tighten.

"Pity my magic only lasts for as long as I'm concentrating on the illusion," Ionie went on. "So it's no use for the competition. But you could use your magic, Lottie. You could climb on to roofs and get rid of any moss and take plastic bags out of the trees and—"

"What if someone saw Lottie? Maybe we should just help without magic," Sita interrupted.

"I suppose," Ionie agreed reluctantly. "But using magic is so much more fun!"

They continued down the road. Sita and Ionie chatted about how they could use magic if only they didn't have to keep it secret but Maia noticed that Lottie was walking a little way behind them.

"Are you OK?" she said, falling back and linking arms with her. Lottie nodded but didn't say anything.

They reached the Copper Kettle café. The door was open and Mary, the cheerful owner, was standing behind the counter with her assistant Rebecca. "Afternoon, girls! What can I get you? Ice cream, I'm guessing?"

"Yes, please!" they chorused, crowding round the ice-cream counter. The different flavours of ice cream looked as colourful as a rainbow.

"Dad's given me enough money for us all to get two scoops," Ionie said.

"Could I have raspberry ripple and

honeycomb, please?" said Maia.

Mary took a double cone and started scooping up the ice cream. "You really do make the best ice cream," Maia told her.

"I have a secret recipe my old Cornish granny gave me – it uses clotted cream," Mary said with a smile. "Everyone always said she used magic as it tasted so good!"

"I bet you've been selling lots with it being so sunny," Lottie said.

"Actually I haven't," Mary said. "It's because of that new holiday and water-sports centre that's just opened down the road. I guess people are going there instead. I'm hoping things pick up in the Easter holidays. It's been much quieter here than it usually is at this time of year."

"If Westcombe wins the Best Kept Village competition, that might help," said Ionie.

Mary nodded. "I'm hoping so. I've tidied up the front of the shop and put out hanging baskets, and I'm going to help tidy up the area around the duck pond at the weekend. The grass is very overgrown there. The fence around the sports field needs repainting as well. Mike asked me to help; he seems keen to get everyone involved."

"Lucia said he really wants us to win this competition," said Maia.

"Well, I hope we do, too," said Mary. She handed Maia her ice cream and then made up cones for Lottie and Ionie. Sita simply couldn't choose – she was hopeless at making decisions – so in the end the others chose for her.

They headed across the main road. On one side was the village and on the other side were woods and the sea. They walked down the small, stony lane that led through the trees to the beach, quickly eating their ice creams before they melted. Ionie's house was at the top of the lane but they didn't stop. They just dumped their school bags in the garden, waved to Ionie's dad and hurried on. They wanted to get to the clearing to see the animals!

Just opposite the footpath that led to the clearing was a pretty thatched cottage where Maia's granny had lived before she died. Maia always felt a flicker of sadness when she looked at it. She really missed her granny but being a Star Friend helped because the magic had shown her that her granny had been a Star Friend, too. Her animal had been a beautiful silver wolf.

"I'm glad Esther's gone," said Ionie,

stopping to look at the cottage. A lady called Esther had bought it at Christmas time but she had been doing some very dark magic. The girls had managed to stop her and get her to leave before she caused too much damage. Now the cottage was for sale again but no one had bought it yet.

"I hope the next person that buys it is normal and nice!" said Maia.

"Come on, you two," said Lottie impatiently, climbing up the small bank and on to the footpath that led to the clearing. It got very overgrown with cow parsley later in the summer but at this time of year it was quite easy to walk down. It twisted and turned through the trees before coming out in the hidden clearing where Maia had first met Bracken.

A stream danced over a small waterfall and headed on merrily through the trees to join the sea. The leaves on the trees were thick and green, and spring daffodils had given way to bluebells and thick clumps of pink-flowered campion that clustered round the tree trunks. Birds sang and squirrels scampered along the branches.

The girls called their animals' names.

"Sorrel!"

"Bracken!"

"Willow!"

"Juniper!"

The Star Animals appeared instantly. Bracken took a flying leap into Maia's arms and nuzzled her neck with his cold black nose. Juniper leaped on to Lottie's shoulder, playing with her hair with his tiny paws and chattering softly. Sorrel twined herself through Ionie's legs, purring loudly, while Willow rubbed her forehead against Sita.

In that moment, Maia felt so happy that she wouldn't have wanted to be anywhere else in the world.

"Is it magic time?" Bracken said eagerly.

"Yep," Maia said, hugging him.

He jumped down and bounced round her legs in excitement, almost knocking Sorrel over. She hissed in annoyance. "Why do you have to be so clumsy, fox?"

"Whoops! Sorry, pussycat!" he said, not looking sorry at all.

Sorrel stalked away. "Ionie, show the others what you've been practising at home." She sat down at a safe distance from Bracken and flicked her tabby tail round her paws.

"OK," said Ionie. "Watch this." She shut her eyes. The air around her seemed to shimmer and then suddenly she wasn't there any more. Instead, they were looking at Mrs King, their headteacher!

"Oh … my… Wow!" gasped Maia.

Sorrel looked smug. "It's good, isn't it?"

"It's amazing," said Sita.

Lottie nodded. "I thought you could only disguise other things. I didn't realize you could disguise yourself to look like another person."

"I only discovered I could the other day," said Ionie. Maia blinked. It was really odd seeing Mrs King standing there but hearing Ionie's voice coming out of her mouth. "At first I could only manage to change part of me into someone else but I've been practising and I've got better at it. Now I just need to learn how to disguise my voice." She transformed back into herself. "It could be really useful if we ever need to spy on anyone."

"Ionie's so clever," purred Sorrel. Ionie tickled her under the chin and Sorrel purred again.

"Maia's clever, too!" said Bracken quickly. "Come on, Maia, show the others how good your shields are getting!"

So Maia opened herself to the current and conjured a shield around herself. The silvery bubble shimmered in the sunlight. Lottie threw pine cones at it and Willow butted it while Juniper scampered up it and bounced up and down on the top but the shield held firm.

"See? Maia's brilliant, too," said Bracken as Juniper jumped off with a flick of his bushy red tail and Maia let the shield fade.

Lottie sighed. "I wish I could do some other kind of magic. Everyone's got extra powers apart from me."

"But being really agile is incredible," said Sita.

"Mmm," said Lottie, not looking convinced.

"Yeah, I wish I could run as fast as you," said Maia.

Juniper scampered up Lottie's leg and on to her shoulder. "Your powers are amazing, Lottie." He stroked her cheek with his paw. "I think they're the best."

Lottie gave a small smile. "Thanks, Juniper." He swung himself into her arms and she cuddled him, hiding her face in his fur.

Maia frowned. For a few weeks now she'd had the feeling that something was bothering

Lottie. She'd seemed a lot quieter than usual.

"How about we have a game of tag?" said Sita quickly. "Us three against you, Lottie. You're too quick for us to play any other way."

"OK then," said Lottie, her eyes lighting up with some of their usual sparkle. "Catch me if you can!" She raced to the other side of the clearing. The others and their animals charged after her but Lottie could duck and dive and swerve faster than anyone. They played chase until they were all exhausted and then practised their magic some more – Sita repairing some bluebells that had been damaged in the game, Lottie practising her climbing and Ionie moving round the clearing, using the shadows to appear and disappear. Maia remembered what she had seen that morning in her mirror and once again tried asking the magic to show her if there was anything they should be worried about.

The same four images fleeted across the surface of her pocket mirror. They didn't make any more sense now than they had then.

"What are you seeing?" Ionie asked, appearing beside her and making her jump. The others came over and listened too as Maia explained.

"I wonder what the magic is trying to warn us about," Maia finished.

"It doesn't sound like it's anything too scary," said Sita hopefully. "A woman looking at herself in a mirror, the main road leading into Westcombe outside the Copper Kettle, some cottages and a TV remote."

"Maybe it's showing the road because it's trying to tell us that someone is coming to Westcombe," said Ionie thoughtfully. "Someone who's going to cause trouble."

Sorrel purred. "Very good thinking, Ionie."

Maia put her mirror back in her pocket. "Well, if something is coming, we'll deal with it like we always do," she declared. "We're Star Friends and anyone who's planning on doing dark magic in Westcombe better watch out!"

Chapter Four

When Maia arrived home, she got changed to go with her mum to Ana and Mike's house.

"Promise me you won't listen if that fortune-teller says you're going to run away with a tall, dark, handsome stranger!" Maia's dad said to her mum as they left.

Maia's mum chuckled. "All right, but can I believe her if she sees great wealth and happiness in our future?"

"Yep, that's fine – you can believe that," said Maia's dad, kissing her and ruffling Maia's hair.

"See you both later. Have a good evening."

They got into the car.

"Do you believe in fortune-telling, Mum?" Maia asked as they drove through the village.

"No," her mum said. "It's just a bit of fun. No one can see the future, Maia."

But Maia knew that wasn't true because *she* could. Not all of it and not always very clearly but she could see some things. A thought jumped into her mind. Maybe this fortune-teller was a Star Friend and really *could* see the future? Or maybe she used a different type of magic, like crystal magic or plant magic, to predict things. Maia felt very curious to meet her.

Ana and Mike lived near to the school in a pretty cottage with a very neat front garden; there were flowers in all the borders and a new bird table. The cottage next door to Ana and Mike's looked very unkempt in comparison – it had ivy scrambling across the walls, a garden that was overgrown with weeds and large clumps of moss on the roof tiles. Maia frowned, feeling that a memory was trying to push itself to the front of her mind. *Ivy…*

But just then she was distracted by the sound of laughing as Josh, Dan and Nikhil came racing down the street on their scooters and started doing tricks.

As Maia's mum parked the car, the door of the untidy house opened and an elderly man stomped out. "Will you boys clear off!" he shouted angrily. "Go and ride those things somewhere else. I'm trying to watch television!"

"Evening, Mr Keeting," said Maia's mum as the boys rolled their eyes and scooted away.

He went inside and shut his door with a bang.

"Oh dear, Mr Keeting really shouldn't have chosen to live close to a school if he doesn't like children playing," said Maia's mum. "The boys weren't doing anything wrong."

Maia followed her mum up Ana and Mike's neat path. Mike opened the door. "Hello, you two – come along in," he said.

"Maia!" cried Lucia, running out of the kitchen as Maia walked into the cottage.

"Why don't you show Maia around, Lucia?" Mike suggested. "Nicky, come and meet Mystic Maureen our fortune-teller. She's in the kitchen."

Lucia dragged Maia all over the house, showing her the large lounge and the study where the fortune-teller was going to see people. There was a table covered with a purple shawl and a large crystal ball in the centre. Maia felt a shiver run down her spine as she looked at it. They had once fought someone who used crystals to do dark magic. It had been very scary.

Next, Lucia took her into the dining room. "Look at all of Nana's dolls," she said, showing Maia a deep window ledge, which had a display of dolls from different countries. They were all shapes and sizes. As well as the two Portuguese dolls, there was a Spanish flamenco dancer in a red dress; a male German doll dressed in knee-length dungarees and carrying a blunt pitchfork; a female doll dressed as an Irish dancer; an American cheerleader holding an American flag; a male French doll with a large plastic baguette in his hands and a string of onions around his neck; and a female doll from Switzerland in an embroidered dress holding a milk churn.

Maia suppressed a shiver as she looked at the glassy eyes staring at her. Maia had always preferred cuddly animal toys to dolls when she was growing up. Ana's dolls were particularly creepy with their old-fashioned clothes.

"Let's go and get a drink," she said, turning away quickly.

She followed Lucia into the bright, spacious kitchen. Mike was taking some sausage rolls out of the oven, while Ana was arranging cookies on a plate.

A red-haired woman who Maia didn't know was standing by the sink. She had a floaty scarf around her neck, a long pink, orange and blue dress, lots of bangles and a necklace made of multicoloured beads that had a silver letter M hanging from it.

"Hi, Maia, this is Maureen the fortune-teller," said Ana.

Maureen gave them a friendly smile. "Are you joining us this evening?"

"No, Maia's here to play with me," said Lucia.

"Are you sure you don't want your fortunes read?" Maureen's light brown eyes twinkled and she pulled her scarf up over her head and suddenly spoke in a mysterious, spooky voice. "I am Mystic Maureen. I can look through the veils of the present and see into the future. Shall I tell you your fortunes, my dears?"

She took hold of Lucia's hand. "Aha, what do I see here? Ice creams and beaches and swimming—"

"But I don't like swimming!" interrupted Lucia.

"I see you watching people swimming then and having lots of fun!" She tickled Lucia's palm, making the little girl giggle and squirm away.

"And you, my dear." Her fingers closed over Maia's.

For a moment Maia tensed. If Maureen really could do magic, maybe she would somehow see Maia was a Star Friend!

"Ah, I spy a handsome boy in your future, and singing and dancing. I can see you like putting on make-up and going to parties." The fortune-teller winked at Maia. "There are no secrets from Mystic Maureen!"

Maia relaxed. It was clear Maureen had no magic at all. Maia never wore make-up and she didn't go to the types of party with music and boys. The only parties she liked usually involved things like swimming or bouncy castles!

"Cookie, anyone?" Ana asked, offering the plate around.

Maureen straightened up, pushing her scarf back. "Well, I won't say no," she said, speaking in her normal voice. She took a bite. "These are delicious!"

"My mother used to bake them for me when I was little," said Ana. "It's an old Portuguese recipe."

"I'd love to have it," said Maureen.

"No problem. I've got it written down – I can photocopy it for you before you leave."

"I showed Maia your dolls, Nana," said Lucia, taking a cookie.

"Dolls?" said Maureen.

"I used to collect traditional dolls when I was little," Ana explained.

"What a coincidence! I love dolls – I collect china ones," said Maureen. "I'd love to see your collection."

"Of course, they're in the dining room. Please take a look," Ana said, showing her to the door. "We'd better get this food through to the lounge."

Maia and Lucia helped carry the food and drinks. People were going to be able to eat and chat there while they were waiting to see Mystic Maureen. When everything was set up, they went into the dining room. Maureen was taking a photo of the German doll.

"Sorry, I hope you don't mind," she said

to Ana, moving the doll back to his position with the others and slipping her phone into her pocket. "I just had to take some photos. They're amazing."

"I don't mind at all," said Ana, smiling. "It's lovely to meet someone else who appreciates them."

"Well, I'd better get ready for my customers," said Maureen, pulling her scarf back over her head and setting off for the study.

There was a knock on the front door. "I'll get it!" called Mike.

"Let's go upstairs, Maia," said Lucia. "I want to show you the bedroom I stay in when I sleep over at Nana and Grandpa's. It's got the bounciest bed ever!"

By the time the evening was over, Maia felt worn out. She'd played game after game with Lucia, helped her get ready for bed and read her five stories. The little girl had only just fallen asleep when Maia's mum called upstairs. "Time to go!"

"Thanks so much, Maia," said Mike as she came downstairs. "It really helped having you here to amuse Lucia."

"No problem," said Maia. She and her mum said goodbye and left.

"So, did you have your fortune told?" Maia asked her mum curiously. "What did Mystic Maureen say?"

Maia's mum laughed. "Oh, nothing much. She said I'm going to go travelling and someone called Raymond is very important to me. But I don't know any Raymonds! It was all very silly but good fun and we raised a decent amount of money for the school." She stifled a yawn. "I'm tired now, though."

"Me too," said Maia. "Looking after a five-year-old is *very* hard work."

As soon as Maia was home, she got ready for bed. When her mum had said goodnight and turned out the main light, Maia called Bracken. He cuddled up to her and she wrapped her arms round him. "It's been a busy day," she said, feeling her eyes starting to close.

He snuggled closer. "This is my favourite part of any day," he said.

Maia smiled sleepily and shut her eyes. "Mine too," she whispered as she fell asleep.

CHAPTER FIVE

"Maia! Wake up!" Maia felt her nose being licked and woke with a start, sitting bolt upright in bed.

"Are you OK?" Bracken asked. He was standing beside her, peering down at her anxiously. "You were tossing and turning and saying, 'Stay back! Go away!' Were you having a nightmare?"

Maia nodded. "It was about Ana's dolls. She's got this big collection of them." She shook her head and tried to clear the nightmare from her mind. "They were chasing me." She shuddered. "It was horrible."

"Do you think it was a magic dream?" Bracken asked anxiously. Although Maia had normal dreams like everyone else, she also had magic dreams, which warned her about dangers that were coming.

"I don't know… No, I don't think so," she decided. "There were no Shades or people doing dark magic. It was probably just a normal bad dream – those dolls were creepy enough to give anyone nightmares."

She yawned and checked her clock. "It's almost morning." She glanced at the crack in her curtains and saw that it was getting light outside. "There's no point going back to sleep."

She lay back and Bracken stretched out on her chest. His whiskers tickled her cheek. "Can we meet and do more magic today?" he asked hopefully.

"We can but Lottie won't be able to join us," said Maia. "She's always really busy on a Tuesday night." She stroked his fur and sighed. "I hope Lottie's OK," she said.

"What do you mean?" asked Bracken.

"I don't know. She just seems a bit quieter than normal. Like something's on her mind."

"Have you asked Sita or Ionie if they've noticed anything?" Bracken asked.

Maia smiled. "Ionie never notices anything."

Ionie had lots of good qualities but being sensitive to others wasn't one of them, although she had been getting better at that since she'd become friends with Maia and the others.

"I'll ask Sita what she thinks. She's always really good at spotting when people are feeling down."

"I hope Lottie's all right," said Bracken.

Maia hugged him. "It may just be me imagining things. Anyway –" she changed the subject – "why don't I get up and see if the magic will show me anything else useful?" She was just pushing back her covers when her phone buzzed. She checked it and saw a message from Lottie.

> Are u all OK? I woke up in the night with a really weird feeling. I felt really scared, like something bad was about to happen. Lxx

Maia replied.

> I'm fine. Mxx

Her phone buzzed again with a message from Sita.

> Me too. Sxxx

Almost immediately Ionie joined in.

And me but OMG! Have u heard about the stuff that happened in the night? The grass around the pond has been cut and the sports-field fence has been painted! No one knows who did it! Isn't that WEIRD?! Ix

Maia gasped as she read the text.

"What is it?" said Bracken.

Maia read Ionie's text out. "I wonder who did those things," she said. "And why at night?"

"It's really strange," said Bracken.

Lottie and Sita sent texts pinging back.

That's so odd! Sxx

Least it's not something terrible! Maybe someone's trying 2 help the village win the contest! Lxx

Maia added her thoughts.

A mystery that doesn't involve dark magic for once. Makes a change! Mxx

She put her phone down. "Perhaps we'll find out more about it at school."

On the way to school, Maia, her mum and Alfie took a detour to look at the sports field. Ana and Lucia were already there, peering at the fence.

"I had to come and have a look when Mike told me about it. I can't believe someone painted it in the night," said Ana.

"And mowed the grass by the pond, too. How did no one see anything – or hear anything?" said Maia's mum as Alfie wriggled to get out of his buggy. "It's like there's been a good fairy in the village! Yes, you can get out for a moment but don't run off, Alfie," she said, undoing the buckles. "It's a real mystery. If they were mowing the lawn by the pond, it must have made a noise."

"But that's the strange thing. Mike said it looks like whoever did it cut the grass by hand with shears. And that's not all – they tidied up Mr Keeting's garden, too," said Ana. "He was very shocked this morning. Mike says it must be someone who wants to help us win the Best Kept Village competition."

Maia's mum shot Ana a look. "It wasn't Mike, was it?"

Ana spluttered with laughter. "Definitely not! I know he wants to win but not enough to go creeping around in the dark and he was definitely in bed beside me all night long."

Maia noticed Alfie picking something up from the grass and lifting it to his mouth. "No, Alfie," she said, running over and grabbing it. At first she thought it was a bottle top. It was made of smooth black plastic and about the right size but it was oval-shaped rather than round. She didn't know what it was. She looked around for a bin but couldn't see one so she shoved it in her coat pocket.

"Come on, in you get again, young man," said Mrs Greene, lifting Alfie back into his buggy. "We'd better get to school."

Lucia held Maia's hand as they walked along the pavement. "Who do you think did all those nice things, Maia?" Lucia asked.

"I don't know," said Maia, mystified. "I really haven't got a clue."

⭐ ⭐ ⭐

Everyone at school was just as baffled. "It doesn't make sense," Ionie said as she and the others walked round the village later that morning. They had been allowed out to put up their posters with their teachers supervising them. "I mean, why would someone do all those things at night? Why not just do them in the day? And why be so secretive?"

"I guess it was someone just trying to do

a good deed," said Sita. "We don't need to worry about it, though. After all, it's not like someone's been doing horrible things."

"I don't like mysteries," said Ionie, frowning. "Hey, Maia, could you use your magic to see what happened last night?"

Maia pulled out her mirror from her pocket. "You three put up the posters in case Mr Neal or Miss Harris come along to check what we're doing while I see what I can find out."

She cupped the mirror in her hand. As the magic current flowed into her, she whispered, "Show me what happened in Westcombe last night – show me the fence being painted." The surface of the mirror swirled and an image of the playing field appeared. Excitement bubbled up inside her. Was she about to solve the village mystery and find out who'd painted the fence?

But she didn't see a person painting the fence – she saw a couple of shapes moving swiftly across the field but they travelled so fast they were just a blur, and then shadows swirled across the image, blocking the picture with darkness. "Oh!" she said in surprise.

"What did you see?" asked Ionie.

"I didn't see anything really, just shadows," Maia said slowly.

Sita's forehead wrinkled. "But I thought you only saw shadows when someone was using a spell to stop people from spying on them with magic."

Maia nodded. "I do."

There was silence as her words sank in.

"So the good deeds last night were done with magic?" said Ionie.

"Not dark magic, though," said Sita anxiously. "It can't be. The things that happened were *nice*."

"Maybe someone is using magic for good," suggested Lottie. "Someone who doesn't want to be found out." She caught her breath, her eyes widening. "You don't think there could be another Star Friend in the village, do you?"

"But wouldn't our animals know if there was?" said Ionie. "Sorrel told me once she could always tell if there were other Star Animals nearby."

"We need to talk to them," said Maia. Her mind was turning everything over. What was going on? Could someone else really be doing good magic in Westcombe?

"We'd better go to the clearing after school," said Ionie.

"I can't," said Lottie. "I've got gymnastics." She sighed. "But you three go. We need to find out what's going on."

"OK, if you're sure?" said Ionie.

Lottie nodded. "I'm used to it."

"We'll tell you what the animals say," promised Sita.

"Girls!" They turned and saw Miss Harris waving to them from the top of the street. "Time to get back to school!"

"Coming!" they called.

They went back up the street and headed past the duck pond with the freshly cut grass around it. It looked much neater, although the ducks were making a bit of a mess on it. Josh, Dan and Nikhil were messing around, picking up grass with duck poo in and throwing it at each other.

Maia saw their posters lying on the ground. "You still haven't put those up!"

"So?" said Dan, stuffing them in a nearby bin. "Who cares? Race you back to school!" he said to his friends and they set off at a run.

"You know, I'm not sure putting the posters up was actually such a good idea," said Lottie, looking around at all the lamp posts with posters flapping from them. "It makes everywhere look a bit messy."

Maia knew what she meant. She had a feeling Mike would be taking the posters down before the actual judging! Still, it had been fun making them.

As Maia and the others got closer to school, they saw Mr Keeting standing in his front garden, talking across the garden fence to Mike. Mr Keeting did not look happy. "It's just not on – people coming into my garden at night," he grumbled, waving his hand at his front garden which was looking much tidier than it had done the day before, with the flower beds weeded and raked over and the grass cut.

"I thought I heard something – strange whispering voices and someone moving around. I should have come out but I was in bed. If I'd known what was going on, I'd have been straight out and given those do-gooders a piece of my mind. They had no right to come into my garden!"

"It's a real mystery but your garden does look better, John," Mike said.

Mr Keeling huffed. "Well, it's still not right," he muttered, shaking his head.

Chapter Six

Maia, Ionie and Sita ran to the clearing that afternoon and called their Star Animals. Bracken, Sorrel and Willow appeared instantly.

"We've really got to talk to you!" said Maia. "Strange stuff's been going on. Last night…"

"Wait!" Willow tensed, her delicate ears pricking. "Someone's coming through the trees over there!"

The animals vanished in the blink of an eye.

The girls looked round. Hardly anyone ever came to the clearing. They saw Mary from

the Copper Kettle walking through the trees.
"Hello, girls!" she said in surprise.

"Hi, Mary," said Maia.

"I'm just getting a breath of fresh air. I've been busy baking cakes all afternoon. I do like walking in the woods if I need to clear my head and this clearing is always so beautiful." Mary smiled. "But don't let me disturb you. You carry on with whatever you were doing."

"It's OK," said Maia. "We'll go down to the beach."

They said goodbye and hurried away. The lane led to a small car park and from the car park a track wound its way down the cliff to the shingle beach. The tide was far out and there weren't many people around.

"Let's go to our secret place," said Maia to the others.

At the base of the cliffs there was a line of big boulders and rocks. In one particular spot, the girls had found a gap between some boulders. Through the gap there was a sheltered circle of pebbles where they could call their animals, shielded from sight by the large rocks. They squeezed through the gap and called their animals' names.

"OK," said Maia as the three animals appeared. "Let's start again!"

* * *

"I don't understand this!" Sorrel stalked round Maia, Ionie and Sita after they'd finished explaining what had been going on. "I don't understand it at all."

"There can't be another Star Friend and Star

Animal nearby," said Bracken.

"We'd definitely know if someone was using the magic current to do Star Magic," said Willow. "We'd feel it."

"So, it's not someone using Star Magic then," said Maia.

"No, but whoever it is must definitely be using some sort of magic if they're blocking you from seeing them," said Bracken.

Sorrel's indigo eyes were suspicious. "Whoever can do that must be able to do powerful magic. I don't like this at all."

"Me neither," said Bracken. They looked at each other in surprise. They weren't used to agreeing.

"What shall we do?" Sita asked them.

"There's nothing much we can do but wait and see what else happens," said Willow.

"Maybe nothing else *will* happen," Sita said hopefully. "Maybe it was just a one-off."

Sorrel sniffed. "Oh no. Someone who can

do such powerful magic is not going to just use it once, and maybe next time they won't use it for good."

Maia cuddled Bracken, a feeling of foreboding running down her spine.

✦ ✦ ✦

When Maia walked to school with her dad and Alfie the next day, they found that all the posters Year Six had put up the day before had been ripped down and stuffed into a bin.

"That's such a mean thing to do," said Maia, feeling upset.

Maia's dad nodded. "Who'd do something so horrible?"

The other parents and grandparents they met on the way in were all asking the same questions and, as they got near to school, they saw a group of people gathered outside Mr Keeting's garden.

They joined the crowd and saw that all the ivy that had been covering Mr Keeting's house had been cut down overnight. There wasn't a single leaf left in the garden, just the stumps of ivy stems at ground level. Mr Keeting was standing in his garden, looking furious. As Maia stared at the ivy on the ground, something stirred in her mind. A memory started to surface but a shout interrupted her thoughts.

"Who did this? Who did it?" Mr Keeting ranted. He pointed at Josh, Dan and Nikhil, who were standing near the fence, nudging each other and pointing. "Was it you three boys? Was it? You're always messing around outside my house."

"No!" Nikhil said quickly. "It wasn't us!"

"Why would we come and cut down your ivy?" Josh said in surprise.

Mr Keeting shook his fist at them. "If it was you boys, you'll be sorry!"

The boys hurried on into school. Alfie started to cry in his buggy.

"Come on, we'd better get going," Maia's dad said.

Maia followed him. Her thoughts were racing. *Who would have cut down Mr Keeting's ivy and taken down all the posters? And why?*

When she and her dad reached the school playground, they found all the Reception children crying. Maia saw Dan, Nikhil and Josh comforting their buddies.

"What's going on?" Maia's dad said, going up to Mike, who was hugging a sobbing Lucia.

Mike looked very unhappy. "In the night, someone came and dug up all the flowers the Reception kids planted yesterday."

"No way!" exclaimed Maia. She'd seen the flower bed the day before, after the Reception children had been out planting lots of summer flowers. It hadn't been the neatest of flower beds but it had been bursting with colour and had looked really pretty. She left her dad and ran round to the Reception block. All the flowers had been dug up in the night just as Mike said! The bed was now just a bank of raked soil and the flowers had vanished.

She saw Ionie and Lottie and dashed over.

"Who'd do such a thing?" she exclaimed.

"It's so mean!" said Lottie.

"I wonder if it was the same person who cut down Mr Keeting's ivy?" said Maia. "Did you hear about that?"

"Yes," said Ionie. "And the posters got ripped down, too. The weird thing is, look how tidy the vandals left the flower bed. You'd think there'd be soil everywhere but it looks like they've brushed it up and even raked it. They also took away all the ivy leaves in Mr Keeting's garden. What vandals do that?"

"That is odd," said Lottie. She shook her head. "And what's also odd is that I woke in the night with a weird feeling again."

"Spooky!" said Maia.

"Juniper said it might be…" Lottie broke off as the bell went. "It doesn't matter."

"We'd better line up," said Ionie. "We can talk more at lunch."

★ ★ ★

First lesson was cancelled because Mrs King called an emergency assembly. She told the children about the events of the night. "This is very serious," she said. "Vandalism is a crime. If anyone knows anything about what happened,

I want you to tell a teacher. We must find out who did this. I really hope no one in this school is responsible."

Maia glanced at Nikhil, Josh and Dan. They were looking as puzzled as everyone else. Despite Mr Keeting's words, she was sure it wasn't them. She'd known them all since playgroup and, although they could be annoying, she'd never known them vandalize anything and she was sure they wouldn't do something that would upset the Reception children so much. She often saw them playing in the playground with their little buddies.

When they went back to their classrooms, Maia hurried into the girls' toilets and shut herself in a cubicle. She'd had an idea. Pulling out her mirror, she whispered, "Show me last night when someone took the flowers from the flower bed."

She saw the flower bed but then dark shadows swirled across it. Her vision was being blocked by magic again!

"Show me Mr Keeting's ivy being cut down," she whispered.

But the shadows continued to swirl. Maia slowly lowered the mirror. So, whoever had done the things in the night had been using magic just like the person the night before! Was it the same person? Surely there couldn't be two other people suddenly using magic in Westcombe? And why would they do helpful things one night and horrible things the next?

She remembered the Reception children crying because their garden had been ruined and determination filled her. Whoever was doing these mean things was going to be sorry.

We'll find out who they are, she thought. *And we'll stop them!*

Chapter Seven

After school, Maia and Sita went to Ionie's house. Lottie persuaded her mum to let her join them after she'd finished her tennis lesson.

"I told her we're doing a project together," she said as they hurried down the lane to the clearing. "It was the only way she'd let me come."

"It *is* a project, only not a school one," said Maia. "It's a magic one!"

They reached the clearing and called Bracken, Sorrel, Juniper and Willow. Today there was no playing. They sat straight down and told the animals what had been going on.

Sorrel hissed as Maia told them how she'd seen nothing but shadows when she had tried to find the culprits behind the night's activities. "We have to find out who's doing these things. I'm sure it's the same person and I'd bet one of my whiskers that Shades are involved."

"It's strange that Lottie woke up feeling like something bad was happening in the night when it really was," said Sita.

"It was probably just a coincidence," said Lottie. "After all, I thought something horrible was happening two nights ago but nothing bad was going on then."

Sorrel gave her a thoughtful look. "There are never coincidences when it comes to magic. I have a suspicion... But no—" She broke off. "For now I believe we should focus on the mystery of what's been happening in the village. We need to find out if Shades were behind these incidents."

"I've had an idea about that," said Ionie. "Why don't I shadow-travel with Sita to the school garden and then we can call you and Willow and see if you can smell any Shades near the flower bed?" Some Star Animals like Sorrel and Willow had the ability to smell when Shades had been around, causing bad things to happen.

"An excellent idea!" Sorrel purred.

"Let's go, Sita," said Ionie. "All the teachers will have gone home by now." She ran to a patch of shadows and held her hand out. Sita joined her and, as their fingers touched, both girls and their animals vanished.

"I wish we could have gone, too," said Lottie.

"I can watch what's happening using magic," said Maia. She took out her mirror. "Show me Sita and Ionie!"

The surface swirled and an image of the school playground appeared. Maia saw Ionie and Sita suddenly appear in a patch of shadows beside the Reception block and look around cautiously. A second later, Sorrel and Willow were there beside them. "They're at school," she said to Lottie. "Sorrel and Willow are sniffing around… Oh!"

"What is it?" Lottie demanded.

"Sorrel's tail just puffed up and Willow's ears have gone flat back," said Maia, frowning. Those weren't good signs.

"I wish I could see what you're seeing," said Lottie in frustration. "You three are all doing things to help and I'm not."

"Well, it's actually Sorrel and Willow who

are helping at the moment," Maia pointed out, watching in the mirror as the animals prowled round the garden. "Ionie and Sita aren't doing much."

Juniper looked at Lottie with his bright indigo eyes. "You might still develop other magic abilities, Lottie."

Bracken nodded. "Yes! Maia only just learned how to make shields and Sita didn't realize she could command people at first."

"And even if you don't end up with any other powers your magic is really good," said Maia.

"Not as good as everyone else's magic," Lottie muttered.

"It is," said Maia.

Lottie heaved a sigh.

"Is something the matter?" said Maia, putting the mirror down and looking at her.

Lottie shrugged. "I guess it just sometimes feels like it's the three of you and then there's me. It's not your fault," she added quickly. "I know you didn't ask to have more magic than me, and I know I can't meet up as often as you three can because of all the extra things Mum makes me do, but sometimes… Well, it feels like I'm on the outside and you're all on the inside."

"But it's not like that at all!" exclaimed Maia. "Don't feel that way!"

"It's not just that, it's… Oh, it doesn't matter." Lottie buried her face in Juniper's fur.

Before Maia could say anything else, Ionie and Sita appeared back in the clearing and called Willow and Sorrel's names. The animals appeared and they all raced towards Maia and Lottie. As they ran over, Maia had to push Lottie's strange words to the back of her mind. She would think about them later.

"It *was* a Shade!" hissed Sorrel. "A Shade destroyed the children's garden!"

"We could smell it really strongly," said Willow, shaking her head and snorting as if she wanted to clear her nostrils.

"That means there's definitely someone doing dark magic again!" said Bracken.

Ionie nodded. "The question is – who? Who conjured the Shade?"

"And why?" said Maia, trying to get her thoughts together. "One night things happen that are nice and helpful, like cutting the grass and painting the fence, and the next night things happen that are horrible and mean. It makes no sense."

"We have to find where the Shade is," said Lottie.

"And what sort of Shade it is," added Juniper. "And who it's affecting."

"Do you think anything will happen tonight?" said Sita.

They exchanged uneasy looks – if it was a Shade, there was no knowing what it would do next!

✦ ✦ ✦

In the morning, the girls woke up to disturbing news. Overnight, bicycles and scooters, slides and climbing frames had all vanished from people's gardens. Children walked to school, crying, with parents looking very cross.

Maia saw Lucia coming out of the house with Mike. He was comforting her. "Don't worry, sweetie. Nana and I will buy you another scooter," he was saying. He looked almost as upset as Lucia did. "Please don't cry."

"Today's a horrible day!" Lucia burst out. "My scooter's gone and Nana's cross with me because one of her dolls' shoes are missing and she thinks I was playing with them without asking but I wasn't."

"It's all right. Don't worry," said Mike.

Maia's mum saw Sita's granny just ahead of them with Sita and Sita's baby brother, Rohan.

"Have you heard about the thefts? I can't believe people didn't see anything," Mrs Greene said, catching up with her. "Surely thieves can't steal all the play equipment in the village and no one hear or see a thing!"

Thieves might not be able to but a Shade could, Maia thought. She met Sita's eyes and could tell she was thinking the same.

"Our neighbours had their grandson's slide stolen," said Sita's granny. "They thought they heard whispering in the garden in the night – in a foreign language, they said. But when they looked out of the window there was no one there and the slide had gone!"

Other people seemed to have similar stories. It was all anyone wanted to talk about. There were no tyre tracks, no footprints and nothing had been captured on any security cameras.

"What are we going to do?" said Maia to

the others at lunchtime. They were sitting in a
quiet spot in the playground.

"We have to find out where the Shade is,"
said Ionie.

"Or Shades," said Sita. "It could be several
of them, like when we fought the ones in the
dreamcatchers and in the stretchy men."

"I can try searching with my magic but
I doubt it'll show anything," said Maia. She
looked into her mirror. "Show me where the
Shades are who have been doing all the things
in the village!" she said hopefully.

But all she saw were shadows.

"Maia, a few days ago, you asked the magic to show you if there was anything we needed to investigate," said Lottie suddenly. "What did it show you? There might have been a clue in those images."

"You saw a TV remote, didn't you?" said Sita. "That was weird."

"Yes, I think so, and the road coming into the village, a woman looking at herself in a mirror and…" Maia frowned. "Yes, that was it, I saw some cottages."

"Whose cottages were they?" Lottie asked.

Maia thought back. "I'm not sure. One had ivy on it."

"Ivy? Like Mr Keeting's cottage – well, before the ivy was all cut down?" said Ionie quickly.

Maia caught her breath. Of course! That's why the ivy on Mr Keeting's cottage had looked familiar to her. "Yes! It *was* his cottage. I can't believe I didn't notice before!"

"Maybe the magic showed it to you because

Mr Keeting is the person behind all of this – perhaps he's been conjuring a Shade?" Lottie said.

"Mr Keeting?" Ionie echoed. "I really can't imagine him doing dark magic."

"And he really wasn't pleased about his ivy being cut down and his garden being tidied up," said Sita.

"He also accused the boys," said Maia. "Surely he wouldn't do that if he was responsible."

"Unless he wanted to trick people," Lottie pointed out.

They all considered it.

"I know how we can find out," said Ionie suddenly. "Try and see him now, Maia. If he's the person doing dark magic, there'll be a blocking spell in place on him, so if you can't see him, we'll know he's guilty!"

"Good idea." Maia got out her mirror. "Show me Mr Keeting," she breathed.

An image of Mr Keeting immediately

appeared. He was sitting in his lounge, watching television.

"I can see him," she said as she saw him take a drink from a mug of tea. "So he can't be the person doing dark magic. He's watching TV."

"TV?" said Lottie suddenly. "The magic showed you a remote control, didn't it, Maia? Maybe there's a Shade in his TV!"

"No! It can't be that," said Maia, letting the magic fade. "We know whoever is doing magic is blocking me from seeing them. But I could see Mr Keeting and his TV just fine."

"Oh." Lottie's face fell. "I thought we'd solved it for a moment."

"Not yet," said Maia, putting her mirror away. "But we will."

CHAPTER EIGHT

"This is ridiculous!" Maia's dad declared as he and Maia stood and stared at the duck pond the next day. All the ducks had been replaced by yellow plastic ones!

"Who can be doing these things?" said one of the other parents.

Maia stared in horror at the plastic ducks bobbing around in the pond. If a Shade was making real birds vanish, then things had gone way too far. She and the others had to sort this out.

"See you later, Dad!" she called and, breaking into a run, she sprinted for school. But as she did so, she trod on something. She stopped and picked it up. It was a small oval piece of black plastic, slightly squashed at the sides. A memory stirred in Maia's head. She'd seen something like this before. Yes, she'd found something similar by the playing field the day after the fence had been painted. Was it just a coincidence?

There are never coincidences when it comes to magic. Sorrel's words echoed in her ears. Maia had been about to put the piece of plastic in the bin but now she hesitated. *Maybe it's a clue*, she thought and she tucked it in her pocket instead.

✦ ✦ ✦

"What do you think it is?" Ionie said, turning the little bit of plastic over in her hands at break time.

"I've no idea," said Maia. "But don't you think it's odd that I found one at the pond and one at the sports field?"

"Definitely," said Ionie, handing it back. "And you know what else is odd? All the streets were swept last night. There isn't a single scrap of litter to be seen."

"What?" Maia stared at her.

"Yeah, I noticed on the way to school. I think everyone else has been so busy wondering what's going on with the ducks that they haven't realized that everywhere is looking really neat and tidy."

"This is just too weird," said Lottie. "So we're looking for a Shade that sweeps the streets and swaps real ducks for plastic ones."

"A Shade that steals flowers and cuts ivy down but who takes the leaves away and rakes the soil over afterwards," said Sita. "What sort of Shade does that?"

"A crazy one," said Maia.

"I've been thinking – you know the cottages you saw with magic?" said Lottie. Maia nodded. "Well, Mr Keeting's cottage might not have been the important thing in that image. Remember when some Shades had been put in dreamcatchers and we were trying to work out where they were? You saw the dreamcatchers in a vision but you didn't realize the vision was showing you the dreamcatchers; you thought it was trying to show you the crystals on the shelf below."

"You're right," said Maia, nodding. "That's a really good point."

"So what else could you see when you saw Mr Keeting's cottage?" said Lottie.

"Mike and Ana's cottage next door," said Maia. "The street outside. That's it, I think, but I didn't get a very good look."

"Well, Mike and Ana can't be the ones conjuring Shades," said Sita. "Neither of them would ever do anything to harm the village or make the children unhappy."

Maia rubbed her head. She had a feeling they were missing something important. "I'll try to see if I can find anything else out with my magic this evening. We're not meeting up, are we?"

"No. It's my brother's birthday so I have to go home," said Sita.

"I've got a flute lesson," said Lottie.

"Mum wants me to go into town to get a new summer coat," said Ionie. "But from tomorrow it'll be the holidays and we'll have much more time to investigate. When I get home tonight, I might do some shadow-travelling with Sorrel and see if I can have a look round the outside of Mr Keeting's cottage, and Ana and Mike's. I might find a clue and I'll see if Sorrel can smell any Shades."

"OK, but be careful," warned Sita. "Whatever you do, don't be seen!"

⭐ ⭐ ⭐

That evening, Maia lay on her bed, cuddling Bracken and thinking everything over. She'd tried asking the magic to show her where the Shade was and who'd been doing dark magic to conjure a Shade but both times all she'd seen were shadows again.

She ran over all the different events in her mind – the helpful things and the mean things that had happened in the village; the strange black plastic objects she'd found and the images the magic had shown her – the cottages, the woman, the remote control. She just didn't see how everything linked together.

"It's like there's something really important that we're missing or just not seeing," she said to Bracken. "Oh, if only we could figure out what type of Shade we're dealing with and what the person who conjured it wants to do."

Her phone buzzed. It was a message from Ionie.

Just got back. Ixx

Maia texted back.

Did u find anything out? M

The next message came back almost in code. The Star Friends tried not to put anything about magic in their messages in case their parents or brothers and sisters picked up their phones and read them.

S could smell Ss near the cottages. The smell was so strong it made her sneeze! I didn't find any clues, though. Everything looked normal. I hope nothing else happens tonight. Ixx

Me too. C u 2moro. Mx

Maia sighed as she put her phone down. The feeling that she was missing something was growing even stronger. Bracken nuzzled her.

"Oh, Bracken," Maia said, hugging him. "I just want to find out what's going on!"

* * *

That night, Maia had a nightmare again. She was standing in the middle of a dark room in a circle of light and she could hear whispers coming from the shadows around her. Fear prickled across her skin. She sensed movement and swung round but whoever it was had moved very fast. A memory stirred in her mind – an image of something moving quickly in one of her visions. The whispers grew louder and she realized the people in the shadows were speaking in foreign languages.

"Come out!" she said bravely. "Stop hiding!"

There was a shifting movement in the shadows and then all the people stepped forwards at the same time.

Maia gasped. They weren't people! They were Ana's dolls and their eyes were glowing red! The German doll was pointing his pitchfork at her; the Swiss milkmaid had her milk churn held threateningly over her head; the American cheerleader was holding her flag as if it was a javelin. The male Portuguese doll stepped forwards, holding his wooden shepherd's crook like a weapon, and the female Portuguese doll raised her fists. Despite her fear, Maia noticed something looked different about her. What was it? Yes! Her black shoes were missing. But, before she had time to think about that, the dolls started advancing on her.

"Bracken!" Maia screamed as the dolls leaped towards her.

She felt Bracken licking her face and woke with a start.

"I was having a nightmare!" she said, pushing her hair back from her face. "It was horrible.

It was about those dolls again."

"Two nightmares about the dolls." Bracken licked her face again. "This has to mean something, Maia. It has to be a magic dream. What were they doing?"

"They were attacking me," said Maia. She shivered and hugged Bracken close.

As she did so, her gaze fell on the two strange bits of black plastic on her bedside table. The female Portuguese doll flashed into her head.

"Shoes!" she gasped suddenly. "The Portuguese doll didn't have shoes on." She grabbed the round plastic objects from her table. "I think that's because *these* are her shoes, Bracken!"

"But why would they be outside, by the duck pond and the sports field?" asked Bracken.

Maia remembered what Mr Keeting and Sita's granny had said about hearing strange voices whispering in the night in foreign languages. Suddenly the missing piece of the puzzle finally fell into place. "Because we're right – there isn't just one Shade," she said. "There are lots of them and they're all trapped in Ana's dolls!"

CHAPTER NINE

Maia wished she could shadow-travel like
Ionie or run as fast as Lottie so she could go
to the others' houses to tell them what she'd
found out and they could work out what to
do next. But all she could do was to send them
a message saying she'd worked out where the
Shades were and wait for them to wake up and
check their phones in the morning.

At 7 a.m. her phone started buzzing like a
bumblebee.

WHAT?!! lxx

What do u mean u know where the Ss are? Lx

Where are they? Sxxx PS Are u OK?

Maia replied.

Yes, I'm OK. Just a bit freaked out. I think they're in Ana's dolls! I need u all to come round here asap. Mx

OK! I'll be at yours at 9! Ix

Me too! Sx

Maia's heart sank when Lottie's message arrived a few minutes later.

I can't come round! I have gymnastics and Mum won't let me miss it. She said I can come over after but don't wait for me. Mum just saw our neighbours out looking for their cat. It went missing in the night! That cd be 2 do with the Shades, too. If you think u can find out what's going on, then just do it. U don't need me. Lx

Maia reread Lottie's last sentence, feeling torn. With everything that had been going on, she'd forgotten she'd been planning to talk to Sita about Lottie. She really didn't want Lottie to feel any more left out but if Lottie was right and cats were now going missing there was no time to waste.

She picked up her phone and typed a message.

OK, but make sure u do come round as soon as u can. We DO need u! Mxxxx

She got dressed, her thoughts racing. Knowing the Shades were in the dolls was a big step forwards. It meant that they knew where to find them so they could send them back to the Shadows. But they still had no idea what sort of Shades they were and who had been responsible for conjuring them and putting them in the dolls. Surely not Ana or Mike? No, Maia simply couldn't believe that. Someone else must have trapped them there for some reason but how had that person done that – and when? Ana had told Maia she'd had the dolls since she was very young.

The unanswered questions raced round

in Maia's head.

"You're quiet," her mum said as Maia sat at the table, barely able to eat even a mouthful of toast. "Are you feeling OK? I thought you'd be happy as it's the first day of the holidays."

Maia shrugged. "I am. I just didn't sleep very well and I'm not that hungry. The others are coming round soon. I'd better tidy my room."

She put the remains of her toast in the bin and hurried back upstairs.

✦ ✦ ✦

At nine o'clock, Ionie and Sita arrived. They rushed up to Maia's room. Shutting her door, they called their animals. It was risky but Maia knew her sister Clio wouldn't get up for a few more hours and her dad had taken Alfie out to the park. Her mum was busy downstairs doing some paperwork so hopefully they wouldn't be disturbed but, just to be on the safe side, she put a chair behind the door to keep it closed.

"So what's going on?" Ionie demanded, sitting on the rug with Sorrel. "What's this about the Shades being in the dolls?"

Maia quickly explained. "I'm sure Ana's dolls have Shades in them," she said. "Sorrel, you smelled Shades outside the cottage, didn't you?"

Sorrel nodded. "Yes, it stank of them."

"So the dolls have been doing all the stuff that's been going on at night – but why?" said Sita. "What sort of Shades are inside them?"

"I don't know," said Maia. She'd been

thinking about it a lot but she still hadn't worked it out. What Shades did both nice things like painting the fence and horrible things like digging up a flower bed?

"Whatever they are, they have to be stopped today," said Sorrel.

"Yes. We need to go to Ana's house this morning," said Ionie. "Then we can send the Shades back to the Shadows."

Bracken leaped up. "Let's go!"

Maia's heart beat with a mixture of fear and excitement as she jumped to her feet, too. They were going to be fighting Shades again!

"Wait!" said Willow. "Is this wise? It sounds like there are quite a lot of Shades if they're in all the dolls."

"So? Sita can use her commanding magic to make them all freeze then I can order them to go back to the Shadows. It'll be easy," said Ionie. Although Sita could command both people and Shades to do what she said, only Spirit Speakers like Ionie could send Shades back to the Shadows. She had to be able to look them in the eye and then, when she commanded them, they would leave the human world.

"But how do we get to the dolls?" said Sita.

"We shadow-travel, of course! Come on!" Ionie ran to a patch of shadows beside Maia's wardrobe.

"Ionie!" Sita protested. "We can't just appear in Mike and Ana's house. What if they're there and see us?"

"Sita's right," said Maia. "We've got into trouble before by rushing into things. I want to go in as well but I think we should be careful."

Ionie hesitated and, for a moment, Maia thought she might just go anyway but then she sighed and stepped out of the shadows. "So what do you think we should do?"

"I think it might be best if we hang around near Mike and Ana's house and wait until we see them go out," said Maia. "Then we can shadow-travel inside and try and get to the dolls."

Ionie looked disgruntled. "All right, we'll do things the slow way if we must."

★ ★ ★

They walked round to Mike and Ana's house. On the way they saw a group of adults gathered round the village sign on the green. The flowers at its base had been replaced with artificial ones in the night.

"Why are the Shades doing these things?" Sita whispered.

"I have absolutely no idea," said Maia.

"To make people argue?" suggested Ionie as they watched the grown-ups start to shout crossly at each other.

"I suppose it could be," said Maia. "The things they've done have made people upset."

"Painting the fence, sweeping the streets and

cutting the grass didn't," Sita pointed out. "And the village does look really tidy."

As they reached Ana and Mike's cottage, they saw Ana coming down the path. "Oh, hello, girls!" she greeted them but Maia noticed her smile wasn't as broad as usual. "You haven't seen a black-and-white cat, have you? My friend's cat disappeared in the night."

"Lottie's next-door neighbour's cat went missing last night, too," said Ionie.

Ana frowned. "I really don't know what's going on in the village at the moment. Mike is beside himself. He's never known anything like this in all the years he's lived here. It's making him ill."

"We'll keep our eyes peeled for the cats," said Maia.

"Thanks." Ana hurried off.

"I wonder if Mike's out, too?" Ionie whispered as Ana disappeared round the corner.

"There's one way to find out," said Maia.

She hurried up the
path and knocked
on the door.

There was a
pause and then
it opened a little
way. Maia saw
Mike inside. "Oh,
hello, Maia," he
said, peering
through the gap. He
looked very stressed.

"I was just wondering if Lucia was here and
wanted to play," Maia said.

"She's at home with her mum and dad," said
Mike. "You could try there. It's Cherry Cottage
on Trinity Lane. Now I've got to go." He
quickly slammed the door shut. Maia frowned.
She'd never known Mike be so abrupt. She
went slowly back to the others.

"Something's definitely going on," she said.

"Mike was acting really oddly."

"Maybe he does have something to do with the Shades," said Ionie.

They walked down the street and sat on a low wall near the stream, pretending to just be hanging out but really watching Mike and Ana's house. After a while, Mike came out, locked the door behind him and hurried off.

"Now can we shadow-travel in?" said Ionie eagerly.

Maia nodded. "All right."

"Let's text Lottie and tell her what we're doing first," said Sita. "Then when she gets home she'll know where to find us."

"We could wait until she gets here before we go in," said Maia.

"But if we do that Ana or Mike might come back," Ionie pointed out. "This could be our only chance."

Maia knew she was right. Pulling out her phone, she sent Lottie a quick message telling her they were at Ana and Mike's and to meet them there.

They all stepped into a patch of shadows at the base of a willow tree.

Ionie grabbed their hands. "OK," she said, her eyes alight with excitement. "Here we go!"

Chapter Ten

Maia always found shadow-travelling a very strange experience. The world seemed to disappear around her and for a moment she had the feeling that she didn't weigh anything. Then her feet touched solid ground and the world returned again. They were standing in Ana and Mike's hallway on the other side of the front door. The door leading to the kitchen was open; the other doors – to the lounge, study and dining room – were shut.

The house should have been quiet but

behind the dining room door they could hear the whispering of strange voices and the sound of movement. The hairs on Maia's arms prickled. Sita squeezed her hand tightly, her eyes wide and scared. Even Ionie looked slightly alarmed.

Maia desperately wanted Bracken. She whispered his name and he appeared beside her. She pressed her fingers to her lips, warning him to stay quiet. He nodded and pressed closer to her legs, his warm body making her feel instantly braver.

A second later, Ionie and Sita had followed her example and Willow and Sorrel were there, too. Sorrel's fur puffed up as she sniffed the air and Willow shook her head as if a bad smell was creeping up her nostrils.

"Shades?" Ionie mouthed to Sorrel.

Sorrel nodded, her indigo eyes deadly serious. She fixed her gaze on the dining-room door.

The hackles on Bracken's neck rose and he lowered his head, his lips curling back over his teeth as he stared at the door.

"We've got to go in there!" Ionie mouthed to the others, pointing to the door.

Sita started to shake her head.

Maia put her lips close to Sita's ear. "It'll be OK. Use your power as soon as we get in," she whispered as quietly as she could.

"After three," Ionie mouthed. "Three … two … one…" She leaped forwards with Maia beside her, reaching for the door handle and pushing the door open.

"Now, Sita!" Maia cried but as Sita burst into the room behind her they all stopped in their tracks. The dolls were scattered around on the floor, lying on the rug as if they were just normal dolls that had been left there after someone had been playing with them.

Maia looked around slowly. What was going on?

"Shades!" hissed Sorrel. "This room reeks of them!"

Bracken snarled and leaped at one of the dolls, his jaws open, but before he could grab it there was a flurry of inhumanly fast movement and all the dolls sprang to their feet. Maia squeaked in alarm as the dolls glared at them, their glassy eyes now glowing red, fists, milk churn, pitchfork and flag raised.

"Whoever you are, you will not stop us!" said the American doll. "No one will stop us from granting a heart's desire!"

"We are Heart's Desire Shades and we make whatever is longed for come true," said the Irish doll. She gave a little giggle. "In our own special way, of course!"

The dolls edged closer, their red eyes full of malice. Bracken growled.

The German doll charged. Sorrel hissed and swiped at him with her claws. The doll spat out a word in German and slashed at her with his blunt pitchfork. With a yowl, she managed to leap out of the way just in time but he was on her in a second, striking at her paws. Bracken snarled in fury and sprang at him, knocking him over. Willow was beside them in an instant, butting the doll hard with her head and sending him flying to the other side of the room where he landed in a heap on the floor.

The other dolls drew in a collective gasp of fury.

Maia turned to Sita, who looked terrified. "Sita! Your magic!"

"F-freeze, dolls!" Sita gasped. Then her voice rose and grew more confident. "All of you! I command you to be quiet and stand still *right now*!"

The Irish and American dolls froze like statues. Only their red eyes flickered angrily from side to side. Maia felt a rush of relief but it quickly changed to horror as she realized none of the other dolls had frozen – they were all still moving!

"M-my magic's n-not working!" Sita stammered.

"It is, but only on two of the dolls!" Willow said, galloping over and lowering her head, preparing to protect Sita as the dolls surrounded them. Their voices rose, their different languages mixing together angrily.

"Try again, Sita!" Ionie urged.

"Be quiet and stand still, dolls!" Sita shouted.

But her words had absolutely no effect. The girls and their animals were backed into a small circle at the centre of the room; Bracken and Sorrel were growling and hissing; Willow was pawing angrily at the ground as the dolls advanced.

Maia opened herself to the magic current, pulling it inside herself just as the Portuguese doll lifted his wooden crook into the air. For a moment Maia saw the other dolls' eyes flicker towards him as if they were waiting for a command. With a yell, he brought his crook down so it pointed at the girls and then he and all the other dolls charged!

Shield! thought Maia. Instantly a silvery bubble formed round her and the others. The dolls rebounded off its surface, yelling in shock as they bounced back and hit the floor in a tangle of arms and legs. Maia concentrated on letting the magic flow through her as she heard Sita and Ionie exclaim in relief.

"Oh, clever girl!" said Sorrel. "That was very quick thinking."

She felt Bracken nuzzle her hand. "You saved us, Maia!"

"For the moment. We can't stay in here forever," said Maia as the dolls got to their feet and started throwing things at the bubble – fruit from the Portuguese doll's basket, onions from around the French doll's neck, the flamenco dancer's castanets and the milk churn.

"What are we going to do?" Sita cried as the German doll leaped at the bubble and started trying to stab it with his pitchfork and the

French doll attacked it with his baguette.

"I know!" breathed Ionie suddenly, pressing her face to the side of the bubble so she could look into the German doll's eyes.

"Return to the Shadows!" she cried. "I am a Spirit Speaker and I command you to return where you belong!"

Maia whooped and waited for the Shade to leave the doll and for the doll to fall lifeless to the floor but it didn't. It just yelled furious words at her in German.

"Go back to the Shadows!" Ionie shouted desperately.

But the doll didn't falter. He clearly didn't understand her. Maia's eyes widened as realization dawned.

"Why isn't my magic working?" exclaimed Ionie.

"They must be using magic to help them block out your words and—"

"No," Maia interrupted Bracken. "It's not

that! They can't be commanded because they don't understand English!"

While the dolls yelled and continued to attack the dome with anything that came to hand, everyone inside it fell silent.

"We need someone who speaks different languages," said Maia above the din.

"Like me?" shouted a familiar voice.

"Lottie!" squealed Sita as Lottie pushed the window open and clambered in.

CHAPTER ELEVEN

Seeing Lottie, the dolls shouted angrily and
began to throw things at her but Lottie was
using her magic and she managed to dodge and
duck all the flying missiles. The German doll
charged at her, his pitchfork stretched out, but
Lottie was even faster. She raced to the other
side of the room in the blink of an eye.

"Lottie! We need to know the word for
freeze or *stand still and be quiet* in German,
French, Spanish and Portuguese!" shouted
Maia. "Don't ask why. There isn't time!"

To her relief, Lottie didn't question her at all. "Um … in German it's *Steht still und seid leise!*" she cried, dodging the pitchfork by jumping up on the sideboard and then leaping right over the top of the silver dome to avoid the enraged French doll.

"*Steht still und seid leise!*" shouted Sita. The German and Swiss dolls stopped in their tracks, frozen in place. Lottie somersaulted over them.

Maia whooped. "What about French?" she cried.

"*Reste-là et tais-toi!*" said Lottie, landing and batting away an onion that was flying at her head. As Sita repeated the words, the French doll fell silent and froze.

There were just three dolls left – the Spanish flamenco dancer and the two Portuguese dolls. They rounded on Lottie. She tried to dodge but the male doll shot behind her and kicked the back of her knees, making her fall over. "I … er … don't know Portuguese," said Lottie, trying to scramble to her feet. "And I've only had one lesson of Spanish!"

The dolls saw her stumped expression and started to laugh, a sinister, evil sound that echoed round the room.

"Wait!" Ionie pulled her phone out of her pocket. "We can find out!"

She started typing into the phone but the dolls' eyes were gleaming wickedly. They leaped at Lottie, the female dolls jumping on to her back, yelling and yanking at her hair. Lottie cried out in pain.

Maia couldn't watch them attack Lottie and not do anything. She let the magic barrier disappear and charged forwards. "Get off her!"

she shouted as Juniper sprang at the dolls, his little teeth bared and his paws outstretched. "Get off her right now!"

The male doll slashed at Juniper with his crook. Bracken and Sorrel raced over, snarling and hissing.

"I've got it here!" yelled Ionie. "I don't know how to pronounce it but I think be quiet and stand still in Spanish is ... is ..."

"*¡Quédate quieta y callada!*" shouted a deep voice. "And it's *fiquem parados e quietos* in Portuguese!"

Maia swung round. Mike was standing in the doorway.

"*¡Quédate quieta y callada!*" Sita pointed wildly at the dolls. "*Fiquem parados e quietos!*" All three dolls jerked to a halt, their red eyes glowing like fire.

"I knew it!" Mike said hoarsely, staring at them. "I knew there was something strange about those dolls. I told Ana I could hear them whispering every night this week, telling me they would grant my heart's desire. Ana didn't believe me but I knew they were the ones doing things around the village. I heard them moving at night!"

He looked at the girls, shock starting to register in his eyes. "What are you four doing here?" Maia tensed as he began to frown. "And where have these animals come from? Why are they—"

"Go to sleep, Mike!" Sita commanded.

He blinked for a second as if he was going to argue and then his eyes closed and he sank to the floor.

"Good thinking, Sita!" said Maia, with relief.

"What's been going on?" demanded Lottie, looking around. "What's been happening?"

"Well…" Ionie began.

"Wait!" Sita interrupted. "We need to send the Shades back to the Shadows first." She motioned to the dolls, standing like statues, their eyes burning with fury.

"Do your stuff, Ionie," said Maia.

Ionie walked up to the American doll, who was nearest to her, and looked her straight in the eyes. "Return to the Shadows!" she commanded.

The doll's eyes glowed even more brightly for a second and then the fire left them and she flopped down, a regular doll once again.

Ionie put her back on the window ledge and then strode over to the Irish doll and repeated the words. The Shade left that doll, too.

"Now for the others," said Ionie. "But we'll need to find out how to say, 'Go back to the

Shadows!' in the different languages."

"Guess this is where we really do have to use the internet," said Lottie, pulling out her phone and typing into it. "Yes, here it is… I've got a translation app to help with my lessons. Here we go. Look at the French doll and say *retourne dans l'obscurité*!"

Ionie did as she said and the Shade vanished. One by one, the Shades were sent away until all the dolls were back on the window ledge, their eyes glassy again instead of glowing red.

"No more Shades!" Ionie exclaimed. "They've gone!"

Maia felt the breath leave her in a rush. Bracken bounded around with Willow. Juniper scampered across the curtain rails in joy and even Sorrel gave a delighted meow.

"So what's been going on?" Lottie demanded again.

They crowded round, telling her everything.

"But who trapped the Shades inside the dolls?" said Lottie. "And what type of Shades were they?"

"We don't know who yet," said Ionie. "It can't have been Mike. Did you hear what he said? He knew there was something strange about the dolls. He wouldn't have said that if he'd been the one who'd put the Shades inside them."

"They told us they were Heart's Desire Shades," Sita told Lottie.

"They were using their magic to make

Mike's heart's desire come true – which I guess was for the village to win the competition," said Maia.

"Everything they did was about trying to make the village as tidy as possible," said Ionie. "But being Shades they did that in ways that would upset people."

"I wonder what they did with the things they took – the scooters, the slides, the disappearing ducks and the missing cats?" said Lottie.

Mike mumbled something in his sleep. The girls looked at him. "We have to get out of here before Ana gets home but we can't just leave Mike on the floor asleep," Ionie pointed out.

"We need to find out if he knows anything more then make him forget all about seeing us and the Shades," said Maia.

"I can do that," said Sita. She glanced at the animals. "But maybe you'd better vanish first just in case my magic doesn't stop him from forgetting about you."

Willow nuzzled her. "Good plan."

"We'll go straight to the clearing after we leave here and call you," Maia said to Bracken. He licked her hand and vanished.

Sita went over to Mike and crouched down beside him, gently touching his arm. Maia saw her breathe in and knew she was connecting to the magic current. "You're going to wake up in a moment," she said to him. "And when you do you will not be surprised that we're here. You're going to answer some questions and when we leave you'll forget everything about seeing us here and all about the dolls behaving strangely. Wake up now, Mike."

Mike's eyes started to blink. Sita helped him sit up. Maia wondered what he would say when he caught sight of them but Sita's magic worked perfectly. He didn't seem surprised to see them but just smiled. "Hello, girls. Goodness, what am I doing down here?"

"You just tripped," Sita said, helping him to his feet. "Up you get."

Mike's eyes widened. "The dolls…" He broke off as he caught sight of them on the window ledge. "I must have had a funny turn. You know I thought the dolls were alive and there were four wild animals in this room." He  shook his head. "Those dolls. All this last week I've been thinking I can hear them talking to me, telling me they'd grant my heart's desire. Then I started hearing strange animal noises from the shed on the cricket pitch this morning. I'd just come back to get

the key to go and find out what was inside."
A worried look crossed his face. "I think I'd
better see a doctor."

"No. There's no need to see a doctor," Sita
said. "Do you understand?"

Mike nodded obediently. "No doctor," he
repeated.

"And you don't need to worry about the
dolls. They're just dolls."

Mike nodded again. "Just dolls."

"Do you have the key to the cricket shed?"
Ionie asked suddenly.

Mike went over to the sideboard and took a
key out of a little bowl.

Sita smiled. "Good. Now why don't you
give that to Ionie and come and sit down in
the lounge and have a nice nap?" She took him
by the arm and led him through to the lounge.
"Sit down and shut your eyes. When you wake
up, you will have forgotten all about seeing us
and the strange noises and talking dolls."

Mike sat down and shut his eyes.

"Sleep now," Sita told him and he started to gently snore.

The girls looked at each other. "Strange animal noises in the cricket shed?" said Ionie, holding up the key. "I think this is something we need to investigate. Time to shadow-travel again!"

She stepped into a patch of shadows by the TV and held out her hands. They all linked fingers and then Maia felt the world fall away.

✦ ✦ ✦

Her feet landed on grass. She opened her eyes to see they were now standing in the shadows behind the cricket shed. It was a very large shed in the corner of the cricket pitch where equipment was stored. A faint quacking was coming from inside.

"Ducks!" she exclaimed.

Ionie ran round to the front of the shed.

She turned the key in the lock and opened the door. In the dim light, they could see slides, scooters, bikes and a group of ducks staring at them with surprised dark eyes. They quacked loudly and waddled towards the open doorway.

"This must be where the dolls put everything!" Maia realized.

The ducks came out into the fresh air, flapped their wings and flew off in the direction of the duck pond, looking none the worse for wear.

From the back of the shed the girls could hear the sound of scratching coming from a large cupboard. Lottie ran over and opened it. Two cats sprang out, looking rumpled and cross. They raced for the door and disappeared across the cricket pitch.

"Poor cats," said Ionie. "At least they weren't in here for too long."

"What should we do about all this play equipment?" Lottie said.

"I vote we just leave it here," said Maia. "We can't possibly return it without people noticing and if they find it here they'll just think it was someone playing a silly prank."

"Good plan," said Ionie. "Let's go to the clearing."

Leaving the shed door open, they shadow-travelled to the shadows in the trees at the side of the clearing. But when they got there they saw Mary from the Copper Kettle sitting on a tree stump.

"How about the beach instead?" whispered Lottie.

They nodded and hurried through the trees and out on to the clifftop. A brisk breeze was blowing and white clouds were scudding across the sun. The girls ran across the windswept grass to the stony path that led down the cliff to the beach. It was deserted. The tide was just starting to go out, the waves pulling back on the pebbles, leaving them shining and damp. The girls headed along the narrow strips of sand and shingle to their secret place. Squeezing in between the rocks, they called their animals' names.

The Star Animals appeared straight away. "So, what happened?" demanded Bracken.

"Did you deal with the man?" said Sorrel.

"Did your magic work?" Willow asked Sita.

"Yes," Sita said.

"Brilliantly!" Maia added.

They told the animals everything.

"One thing I still don't get is how you suddenly appeared, Lottie," said Ionie.

"I was just getting in from gymnastics when I read Maia's text and at the same time I got one of my horrible feelings but it was worse than all the others I've had. It made me feel really worried. I tried to text you back, Maia, but you didn't reply. I knew that was odd because you nearly always reply straight away so I decided to use my magic to run to Mike and Ana's. I was having a look round the house to see if I could find you when I heard voices coming from the open window. I peeped in and saw what was happening…"

"And then saved the day," Sita finished.

Maia hugged Lottie. "Thank you!"

"I don't know why I had such a strong feeling something was wrong," said Lottie. "But I'm glad I did."

"I believe you're developing a new power, Lottie," said Sorrel, fixing her with a thoughtful look. "I believe you're developing the ability to sense when dark magic is threatening people nearby."

"I agree with Sorrel," said Juniper. "I told you I thought something like that might be happening."

"I know but I didn't quite believe it." A smile lit up Lottie's face. "This is awesome! With a power like that, I'll be able to really help fight dark magic."

"You help already," Maia told her quickly. "Your agility magic is amazing. If it hadn't been for that, you wouldn't have got to us in time…"

"You wouldn't have been able to climb in through the window so quickly," said Sita. "Or dodge the dolls."

"And it's not just your magic that we need," said Ionie. "We need your brains. None of the rest of us knew the foreign words to stop the dolls."

"And you were the one who realized that, though I thought the magic was showing me an image of Mr Keeting's house, it could be that we were supposed to be looking at something else in the image. I should have been looking at Mike and Ana's cottage," Maia reminded Lottie. She hugged her. "You're brilliant in so many ways. We couldn't possibly manage without you!"

Lottie glanced around tentatively. "So, when

we go to secondary school, you won't decide you don't need me any more and that the three of you want to be Star Friends without me?"

They stared at her.

"Of course not!"

"No way!"

"Why would you think that?"

Lottie looked a bit embarrassed and picked at a fingernail. "I don't know. It's just I've been thinking about how we're going to be at different schools and how weird that'll be," she admitted. "Everything's going to change."

Sita took her hand. "It will be strange being at different schools but we'll always be best friends."

"Always," said Maia. "That won't ever change."

It was as if a heavy weight had been sitting on Lottie's shoulders and it was now suddenly lifted. Her eyes shone as she looked at them. "I've been so worried about it!"

Ionie frowned. "Lottie, for someone who's really clever, you can be really dumb at times. We're best friends and that's that."

Lottie smiled. "So what do we do next?"

"Well, first we need to work out who put those Shades in the dolls," Ionie said.

"And we have to figure out why the magic showed a picture of a woman looking in a mirror and a TV remote," said Maia. "They may be important clues." She glanced up. The clouds had cleared from the sky and the sun was shining down. "But we've got the whole holidays to work on that. Right now, I think we should have some fun! I want an ice cream but first – who wants to paddle?"

"Me!" they all said apart from Sorrel.

Maia pulled off her socks and shoes and squeezed out between the boulders. The beach was still deserted. She ran towards the water, the shingle digging into her toes.

Bracken yapped and bounded past her to the water's edge. Juniper and Willow quickly followed with the girls while Sorrel picked her way very cautiously across the wet stones, stopping every now and then to shake a paw.

Bracken leaped into the water, jumping around with Willow, while Juniper scampered about at the edge of the waves and Sorrel stood some way off. The girls rolled up their jeans and paddled into the water, too.

"Come and play, pussycat," Bracken said,

bounding out towards Sorrel.

She arched her back. "You're wet! Stay back!"

Bracken shook himself, covering her with water droplets.

She hissed and leaped back. "I'll get you for that, fox!"

"Have to catch me first," Bracken said cheekily.

Ionie grinned and ran over to pick Sorrel up. "Don't worry about him, Sorrel," she said. Looking slightly happier, Sorrel purred and cuddled up in Ionie's arms.

"Isn't this wonderful?" said Lottie, turning her face upwards. "I love the sunshine."

"I love holidays!" said Sita happily, linking arms with Lottie. "Beach trips, ice creams, seeing friends and…"

"Having exciting magical adventures!" finished Maia. She spun round in the water, happiness filling her as she watched Bracken,

Willow and Juniper playing in the sparkling waves while her friends laughed, their faces lit up by the golden rays of the sun.

About the Author

Linda Chapman is the best-selling author of over 200 books. The biggest compliment Linda can have is for a child to tell her they became a reader after reading one of her books. Linda lives in a cottage with a tower in Leicestershire with her husband, three children, three dogs and three ponies. When she's not writing, Linda likes to ride, read and visit schools and libraries to talk to people about writing.

www.lindachapmanauthor.co.uk

About the Illustrator

Lucy Fleming has been an avid doodler and bookworm since early childhood. Drawing always seemed like so much fun but she never dreamed it could be a full-time job! She lives and works in a small town in England with her partner and a little black cat. When not at her desk she likes nothing more than to be outdoors in the sunshine with a hot cup of tea.

www.lucyflemingillustrations.com